KU-705-902

Ahoy matey! This here top secret pirate book of sea monsters is filled with tales of me adventures all across the seven seas— both as a pirate and an Octonaut. Keep this book with ye on yer travels, and ye'll be ready for any monstrous encounter! Now read on, if ye dare...

Yours truly, Kwazii

THIS TOP SECRET BOOK
IS THE PROPERTY OF:

_____

**FOR
CAT PIRATES
ONLY!**

L.B. OF HACKNEY
91300000926544

KWAZII'S PIRATE BOOK OF SEA MONSTERS

The Eight-Headed Sea Monster

Whoever said eight heads were better than one never crossed paths with the Eight-Headed Sea Monster! There are many tales about this sea-monster – but this is the one all cat pirates know. Long ago, a proud ship sailed across the sea. Along with its mighty crew, the ship carried a precious golden jar. But a terrible storm sank the fine ship to the bottom of the sea. There the golden jar lay…until a terrible beast made the wreck his home! The Eight-Headed Sea Monster! But he didn't scare me! With an old map I found the shipwreck and the jar, and that's when the monster snuck up behind me…

Turn the page matey – if you dare!

OCTOPUS

And it turned out to be an eight-tentacled OCTOPUS!
This octopus was as amazing as any magical sea
monster. When Dashi tried to take his picture, he
vanished by changing colour so he looked just like
a rock! Plus he could squirt ink and squeeze into
tiny spaces, because he had no bones. Turns out the
octopus was great at hide-and-seek, and his favourite
hiding place was the long lost golden jar!

The Vampire Squid

Any pirate brave enough to travel down to the bottom of the sea knows to beware of the dreaded Vampire Squid! They say he lives in a castle in the deepest, darkest corner of the Midnight Zone. And that he has a big cape covered in sharp spikes, plus eyes that glow in the dark! And if ye get too close to him, he squirts a horrible slime all over you as his tentacles draw you closer! How do I know? Because one day, not so long ago, Peso, Captain Barnacles and I came face to face with…

...the VAMPIRE SQUID! 'Tis true we never saw a castle, but the Vampire Squid's as real as you or me, matey! He had spikes and a web between his tentacles – just like a cape! And most amazing of all, he had two lights on the top of his head that he could turn on and off. They looked just like glowing eyes! Oh, and that horrible slime? That's real too! But turns out he just shoots it at you if he's scared!

VAMPIRE SQUID

The Duck-Faced River Monster

Pirates often whisper of a strange beast said to lurk in the murky depths of Australian rivers. It's made up of parts from different creatures: a duck's bill, a bear's fur, an otter's webbed paws, a cat's claws, a beaver's tail and worst of all – a sharp, spiny stinger, like a giant bumblebee! It only comes out at night but it can always find you in the dark, and when it does – yeow! As it so happens, the last time the Octonauts were in Australia we were trying to find Peso's medical bag on a dark river bed, when Shellington got stung by some shadowy beast! I knew it could only be the work of the Duck-Faced River Monster...

DUCK-BILLED PLATYPUS

Unless of course it was a DUCK-BILLED PLATYPUS!
Which it was! Platypuses are river animals who only live
in Australia and look like a bunch of different creatures
mixed together including a duck with their bills. Speaking
of bills, theirs are very special and let them sense things
in the dark. They even found Peso's lost medical bag! The
females lay eggs and also the males have stingers on
their back legs. He only stung Shellington because he was
protecting their egg - which hatched right in front of us!
Out came the cutest little nipper I ever did see.

The Ghost Pirate

Pirates are the best at sneaking - through shipwrecks, around sleeping sea monsters, into the kitchen for a late night snack... But the sneakiest pirate of all is the Ghost Pirate! Able to make anything disappear with a touch of his paw, the Ghost Pirate can creep up on you and steal your whole treasure chest before you can even say "Yeow!" One night, we heard strange sounds in the Octopod and things started to disappear - including me spyglass! To get it back, I knew I had to out-sneak the sneakiest of pirates...

It turns out the Ghost Pirate is not the sneakiest creature in the seven seas! That honour goes to the DECORATOR CRAB! He took objects from all over the ocean – and the Octopod – to use for camouflage! By covering his shell with seaweed, shells and other stuff, he can hide from predators, like sharks, that want to eat him. Camouflage helps him blend in and disappear! He didn't know some of the stuff was ours. So once he gave back me spyglass, we helped him cover up with a seaweed disguise!

The Nackawack

Aaargh, the Nackawack! Just saying it's name sends shivers down me whiskers! This slippery sea serpent is as long as three whales set end to end. Each of its teeth are the size of a dolphin. And he's crafty matey! He likes to knock over ships just for the fun of it. It's why he's one of the most dreaded monsters of the deep. And one day, we caught sight of one through the window of the Octopod, ready to strike...

13

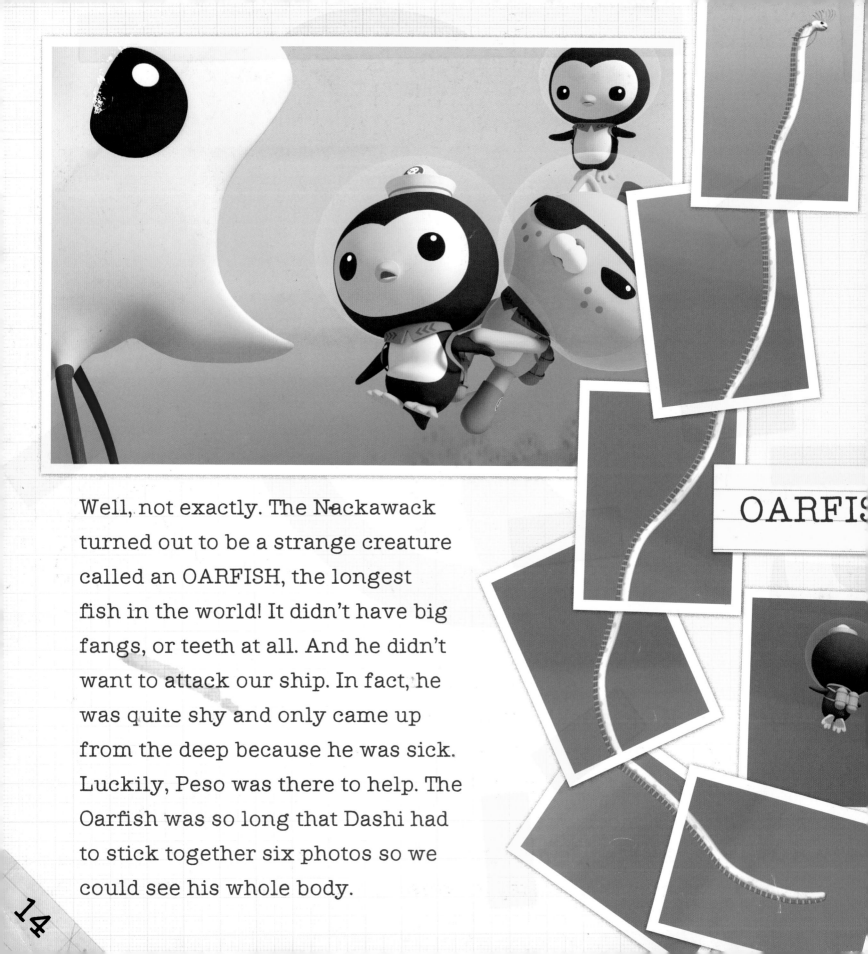

Well, not exactly. The Nackawack turned out to be a strange creature called an OARFISH, the longest fish in the world! It didn't have big fangs, or teeth at all. And he didn't want to attack our ship. In fact, he was quite shy and only came up from the deep because he was sick. Luckily, Peso was there to help. The Oarfish was so long that Dashi had to stick together six photos so we could see his whole body.

OARFIS

The Tri-Toothed Terror

This monster has three gigantic teeth and is feared by all who sail the seven seas. The Tri-Toothed Terror is huge and fierce, and sneaks up on ships and bites 'em in half. Then he just disappears - all that's left is bits o' driftwood and just a whiff of his bad breath! There's been many a good ship lost to this toothy beast! I know this matey, because one day it happened to me...

Well, sort of. The Tri-Toothed Terror turned out to be a far smaller creature called a COOKIE CUTTER SHARK. This pesky nibbler and two of his mates bit into the Gup-A not so long ago, and one of 'em left all of their teeth behind! They do that sometimes, as well as eat their own teeth for vitamins! But mostly they love biting into a whale's blubber, and usually just leave perfect little holes behind. Avast, Cookie-Cutters! Stay away from the Gup-B!

The Sea Ghost

Me hearty, if you be scared of ghosts then you should be ten times as scared of a Sea Ghost! If ever you're unlucky enough to meet one, first you'll hear a spooky whisper. Then you'll feel something crawling on you. And finally you'll see it – an eerie white beastie, with pale, slimy arms stretching out from its body like long, squirmy eels, ready to grab you! Peso and I were exploring a shipwreck one day, when we heard a ghostly whisper. Peso screamed as something grabbed him...

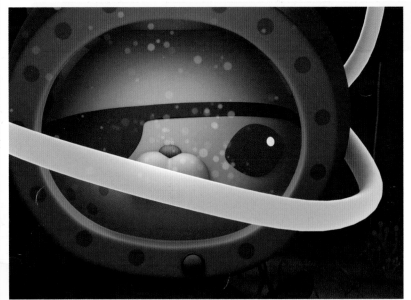

LONG ARMED SQUID

But the thing that grabbed Peso wasn't a Sea Ghost – it was a LONG ARMED SQUID! There are lots of different kinds of squid in the sea, but this is the only one with tentacles that have elbows, just like in your arm! The Long Armed Squid wasn't trying to attack us. In fact, he was very shy and usually likes to hide in the old wreck. He just needed help with a stuck tentacle. But beware! You never know what you'll find in a sunken shipwreck...

The Magical Flying Swords

According to one of the oldest cat pirate tales, on the night of the rare Pirate Moon, when cold ocean waters turn warm, ye may be lucky enough to see the Magical Flying Swords! They're a sign you are near a special sunken pirate ship, where you'll find the greatest treasure ye could ever hope to see...the golden Sword of the Pirate King! But me hearties, if you find the treasure...beware! 'Tis guarded by the three Magical Flying Swords! I should know, I once battled those very same Magical Flying Swords...

SWORDFISH

...which turned out to belong to three SWORDFISH! The swordfish use their noses to defend themselves, just like a swordfighter. The water was warm because they can heat up their eyes to see better in the dark. A handy trick for any pirate or swashbuckler! Once we stopped fighting, we became fast friends and they even let me take the Pirate King's sword! I keep it in me treasure chest back home on the Octopod.

The Monster of Creepy Cove

There's a strange creature known only to pirates as...the Monster of Creepy Cove! This monster can change colours, like magic! It can make itself grow as big as three whales! And as if that's not scary enough, it can make perfect copies of itself until you're surrounded on all sides by creepy monsters! Most pirates stay away from Creepy Cove if they know what's good for them. But I'd always wanted to explore it and see that monster for meself. So that's just what I did! And you'll never believe what I found...

Well, you might believe what I found, because it was real – a CUTTLEFISH! A cuttlefish is related to an octopus and can do amazing things! Like change his colour to hide amongst rocks. Or scare away bigger fish by blowing himself up to look like a giant! Or even squirt out ink shapes that look like more cuttlefishes! Avast! That cuttlefish was trickier than the trickiest cat!

The Giant Shrimp Monster

If ye think all shrimps are small...think again! The Giant Shrimp Monster is so big it makes even whale sharks look shrimpy! If you've ever heard a thunderous boom in the distance...chances are there's a Giant Shrimp Monster somewhere snapping its beastly claw. The sound it makes is so loud it sends even the bravest adventurers into a deep trance. One time, the other Octonauts met this monster and were put into a trance by its massive snap...

SNAPPING SHRIMP

Though, it wasn't really a monster. And it wasn't really giant. But it was a shrimp – a SNAPPING SHRIMP. You see, she thought the Octonauts wanted to eat her. I told her Octonauts don't eat sea creatures. We help them! When the Octonauts woke up, we all put on ear protectors and the shrimp showed us how she made her loud snap; her big claw opens and actually makes a bubble, and when it pops – BOOM! That's how a little Snapping Shrimp makes one of the loudest sounds in the ocean!

The Ghost Whale

On dark nights, when cat pirates like to sail the most, you must always remember to keep an eye out for the strangest of beasts – The Ghost Whale! It looks like a whale to confuse you, but it be a sea monster, as pale and cold as the moonlight! It's crafty as any pirate that ever lived. It only rises from the depths at night to play tricks on passing ships, sending them onto dangerous rocks. Even the bravest pirates fear this ghostly creature. One night on the Octopod, I heard a loud moan and spotted something pale white outside. I was sure it was the Ghost Whale…

But no! The Ghost Whale turned out to be an ALBINO HUMPBACK WHALE! A very rare whale with white skin. There aren't many of these in the world, matey! His skin was so pale he had gotten a bad case of sunburn when he swam up to the surface to get air. Luckily, I knew we could use mushroom coral as sun lotion to soothe and protect his skin. I still hope to spot a Ghost Whale one day. Until then, I count myself lucky to have spotted the rare albino whale!

The Sea of Vanishing Ships

There be parts of the oceans that all pirates stay away from. One of them is the Sea of Vanishing Ships! Many a good pirate has entered and never returned. They say it's sea monsters that made 'em disappear… slimy seaweed creatures with long, stringy fingers that like to take what's not theirs, especially ships! And gups! Even Octonauts! Not long ago, Captain Barnacles, Peso and I took the Gup-X into the Sea of Vanishing Ships…

LOGGERHEAD SEA TURTLE

And er...we got lost! Really lost! It turned out the sea of vanishing ships was a huge patch of seaweed infested ocean called the Sargasso Sea. Luckily, we met a friendly LOGGERHEAD SEA TURTLE in there! Peso bandaged his fin and he helped us find our way out of that mucky maze of seaweed. Loggerheads have an amazing sense of direction, matey, over thousands of miles! He's a good pal for a lost pirate – or Octonaut – to have!

The Ice-Fanged Chomper

Pirate legend tells of a rare sea-beast that lives under the ice in Antarctica, with teeth like razor-sharp icicles! The sneaky scallywag swims under your feet and chomps the ice right out from under you! That's why most pirates steer clear of Antarctica. If the cold doesn't get you, the Ice-Fanged Chomper will! But I'm not most pirates! I recently travelled to Antarctica with the Octonauts and we found a mysterious hole in the ice. As we gazed down into it, a dark shape suddenly darted into view...

WEDDELL SEAL

Was it the Ice-Fanged Chomper? Well, no, it was not. But it was an amazing cold-water creature called the WEDDELL SEAL! Her name was Wilma, and she needed to come up to the surface to breathe. But the ice hole had frozen over! Wilma was trapped! We helped her break through the ice, so she could take a deep breath, and then Peso fixed her broken tooth. So now she can chomp a new breathing hole wherever and whenever she wants. Antarctica's a cold place matey, but if ever you find yourself there, expect a warm welcome from Wilma the Weddell Seal!

Be on the lookout for sea monsters until the next adventure, me hearties!

{KWAZII}

JOB

Lieutenant of the Octonauts

FAMILY

Grandad – the Great Pirate Calico Jack

SPECIALITY

Swashbuckling and acts of derring-do

SIGNATURE GEAR

Eye patch and spyglass

FAVOURITE GUP

The Gup B – it's super speedy!

FEARS

None! Er…except spiders!

SIMON AND SCHUSTER · FIRST PUBLISHED IN GREAT BRITAIN IN 2014 BY SIMON AND SCHUSTER UK LTD, 1ST FLOOR, 222 GRAY'S INN ROAD, LONDON WC1X 8HB
A CBS COMPANY. KWAZII'S PIRATE BOOK OF SEA MONSTERS © 2014 SILVERGATE MEDIA LTD. · OCTONAUTS ™ OCTOPOD ™ MEOMI DESIGN INC.
OCTONAUTS COPYRIGHT © 2014 VAMPIRE SQUID PRODUCTIONS LTD, A MEMBER OF THE SILVERGATE MEDIA GROUP OF COMPANIES. ALL RIGHTS RESERVED.
ISBN 978-1-4711-2066-4 · PRINTED AND BOUND IN CHINA · 10 9 8 7 6 5 4 3 2 1 · WWW.SIMONANDSCHUSTER.CO.UK

MORE AMAZING ADVENTURES!

OCTONAUTS and the Flying Fish

OCTONAUTS and the Whale Shark

OCTONAUTS The Amazing Octopod
A Pop-Up and Play Adventure

OCTONAUTS and the Giant Squid

OCTONAUTS and the Undersea Eruption

OCTONAUTS Deep Sea Octo-Lab Sticker Activity Book

OCTONAUTS Pirate Playtime Sticker Activity Book

OCTONAUTS and the Orcas

OCTONAUTS and the Whitetip Shark

OCTONAUTS and the Monster Map
A Lift-the-Flap Adventure!

OCTONAUTS Desert Island Doodle and Sticker Book

OCTONAUTS to the Rescue!
Sticker Scene Book

OCTONAUTS CREATURE REPORT

OCTONAUTS and the Marine Iguanas
A Lift-the-Flap Adventure!

OCTONAUTS Octopod Adventure
Drive the Octopod through the ocean deep!

OCTONAUTS Meet the Crew

OCTONAUTS Search and Find

OCTONAUTS Go Go Gups!

OCTONAUTS and the Great Christmas Rescue!

OCTONAUTS Ready for Action in the GUP - A!

OCTONAUTS Ready to Race in the GUP - B!

OCTONAUTS and the Great Penguin Race

OCTONAUTS Little Library

OCTONAUTS and the Decorator Crab

OCTONAUTS and the Colossal Squid

OCTONAUTS and the Very Vegimal Christmas!

OCTONAUTS and the Electric Torpedo Rays

www.theOctonauts.com

www.simonandschuster.co.uk